Supersonic Warrior vs the Shopping Carts

Josh Zimmer

Cats are cute and fuzzy! They are entertaining to watch, and have fun!

DEDICATION

Dedicated to Echo, my fuzzy black cat in real life that inspired me to write this short story. He is soft, cuddly, and fun to snuggle with. His fur shines in the darkness.

The short story is inspired by various fantasy and superhero elements. I love superheroes and fantasy. Fantasy is an cool genre, because of the cool worlds and creatures. Superheroes are cool as well, with their amazing worlds, elements, and characters.

CONTENTS

ACKNOWLEDGMENTS

Echo – for being an cute and fuzzy inspiration for the story

Marvel Studios and Power Rangers- for inspiring the powers and characteristics of Supersonic Warrior

Stan Lee- for inspiring the creation and gadgets of Supersonic Warrior

Christina Zimmer- for inspiring the story by rescuing Echo from the grocery store shopping carts.

The short story will teach readers how to be brave and courageous to rescue hopeless animals, since the world is an scary and unsafe place for animals of all types. Animals don't know how to react to real life situations like humans do, since animals have an different genetic system and respond to situations differently.

SUPERSONIC WARRIOR SAVES THE DAY

On an stormy night, an car was speeding through the city with rain drops hitting the windows. An small black kitten was in the back seat of the car, with his paws outside the window. The car hit an bump and an lightning bolt hit the car. Echo, the small black kitten, got spooked and fell out of the window into the parking lot of an grocery store called World of Food. The parking lot was filled with scary cars zooming everywhere. Echo got scared and ran towards the vending machine. Echo got to the vending machine, and he started whacking the buttons on it. The machine shook and he got scared, and ran behind the vending machine. Echo was cowering in fear behind the machine and he was crying in meows. He was so scared! He was in an new world and he didn't know what to do. The night got even worse for him though! The shopping carts came alive, and started growling and howling. The shopping carts pounced while growling into the vending machine. The vending machine fell over and spooked Echo! Echo was terrified and he was cowering in fear. The shopping carts were about to tear him apart and Echo was too scared to respond. World of Food was about to close down for the night, and the employees looked out the window. The employees saw the commotion outside. Justin, one of the World of Food employees, tapped Christina on the shoulder and said, "You should probably help the kitten outside, our shopping carts are about to tear him apart." Christina said, "I agree, the kitten will get badly injured." Christina went outside towards the vending machine. Christina stopped at the vending machine, and saw the growling shopping carts with the terrified black kitten. Christina jumped into action! She took out her superhero device and yelled out "Lets Go Supersonic!" An explosion of rainbow energy surrounded Christina and she transformed into Supersonic Warrior. Supersonic Warrior charged into the shopping carts and knocked them into the air. She roundhouse kicked them into the vending machine. The shopping carts got mad and growled in anger. Echo was terrified and hid in the corner. The shopping carts pounced at Supersonic Warrior, and bit her on the arm. Their fangs were attached to her arm, and the shopping carts shook Supersonic Warrior and threw her into the air. One of the shopping carts jumped in the air and kicked Supersonic Warrior in the chest. Supersonic Warrior was sent flying into the side of the grocery store. The shopping carts grinned and walked closer to their prey as the Supersonic Warrior laid next to the wall. The shopping carts pounced at the Supersonic Warrior, but she outsmarted them. Supersonic Warrior punched them backwards with an Lightning Punch from her arm. One of the shopping carts were defeated and disappeared into dust, but his buddy didn't like that. The other shopping cart got super mad and howled. The shopping cart powered up from his howling and an aura of red energy surrounded it. The shopping cart grinned with his fangs out, and he zoomed straight at Supersonic Warrior. Supersonic Warrior responded with an roundhouse kick. The shopping cart dodged and countered with an flying punch. Supersonic Warrior fell back and rolled on to the ground. The shopping cart opened his mouth, and blew super hard to create an huge gust of wind. Supersonic Warrior took out her sword and threw it like an boomerang at the shopping cart. The sword hit the shopping cart on the side of his head, and the shopping cart screamed in pain. The shopping cart regained his thoughts, and he shot out an energy beam from his mouth. Supersonic Warrior summoned an energy shield with her sword to block the energy beam. The shopping cart's aura powered up the energy beam, and the beam grew bigger. Supersonic Warrior said an enchantment by shouting, "Supersonic Enchant!", and the energy shield got enchanted, and deflected the energy beam back into the shopping cart. There was an huge explosion when the energy beam hit the shopping cart. The explosion smashed Supersonic Warrior into the grocery store, that shattered multiple windows, and the shopping cart got pushed back an couple of feet, and he was enraged. The fangs on the shopping carts sharpened as the Supersonic Warrior got up and was catching her breath. The shopping cart zoomed at Supersonic Warrior. Supersonic Warrior rocket kicked the shopping cart into the air. The shopping cart smashed into the ground, and evaporated into dust. The dust cleared and Supersonic Warrior breathed an sigh of relief as she was brushing the dirt and dust off of her suit. Echo was hiding behind the vending machine, trying to hide himself with his paws. Supersonic Warrior walked to the vending machine and bended down to comfort the kitten. Supersonic Warrior said calmly, "It's ok, little buddy, I won't hurt you. I am not with the scary monsters, I am an friendly superhero, it is my job to make sure that you are safe." Echo walked closer to the Supersonic Warrior, and started growling. Echo had an stressful life, and didn't like trusting strangers. Echo pounced and grabbed Supersonic Warrior's arm.

Supersonic Warrior screamed in pain as Echo started using his claws on her. Supersonic Warrior calmed down, and thought, "If I calm him down, The pain will go away." Supersonic Warrior started petting Echo and he stopped scratching her arm. Echo leaped off of her arm and started purring. Supersonic Warrior said an spell, "Supersonic Cat Food!", and summoned an can of cat food with her sword. She opened it up for Echo to snack on. Echo munched on the cat food and was purring happily. Supersonic Warrior demorphed in an flash of rainbow energy! Christina comforted Echo and was petting him. Echo was smiling while he was munching his cat food. Christina walked over to her car and opened it up. She got out her cat carrier and walked back to Echo. She set the cat carrier down in front of Echo. Echo was interested, and he started smelling and checking out the cat carrier. Christina said, "I am going to take you home, little buddy. The world is unsafe for you!" Echo was interested, and he started whacking at the cat carrier. Christina opened the cat carrier, and locked Echo inside. She walked to her car with the cat carrier. She opened the car, and put the cat carrier in the back seat. Christina started up the car, and drove out of the parking lot. Echo and Christina drove off into the sunset back to their house.

ABOUT THE AUTHOR

Josh Zimmer is an crazy individual with an extreme imagination. He loves to have fun by listening to music, writing stories, and playing video games of various genres such as platforming, multiplayer online games, role playing games, and sports games. His favorite technology brands are Nintendo and Microsoft. They are wonderful role models for the industry. He commands an army of cats to his will with hugs, love, and snacks. He makes the cats purr and meow with happiness.

Josh Zimmer

Supersonic Warrior vs the Shopping Carts

Supersonic Warrior vs the Shopping Carts

Supersonic Warrior vs the Shopping Carts

Supersonic Warrior vs the Shopping Carts

Josh Zimmer

www.ingramcontent.com/pod-product-compliance
Lightning Source LLC
Chambersburg PA
CBHW072305130726

47910CB00012B/2535